This book belongs to

First published 1987 by Macmillan Children's Books
a division of Macmillan Publishers Limited
25 Eccleston Place, London SW1W 9NF,
and Basingstoke.
Associated companies worldwide

This revised edition published 1995

ISBN 0 333 64760 2

Copyright © 1980 and 1995 Jill Murphy

9 8

A CIP catalogue record for this book is available
from the British Library

Printed in Hong Kong

PEACE AT LAST

JILL MURPHY

MACMILLAN
CHILDREN'S BOOKS

For Graham
and Caroline
and their
children.

The hour was late.

Mr. Bear was tired
Mrs. Bear was tired
and
Baby Bear was tired. . .

. . .so they all went to bed.

Mrs. Bear fell asleep.
Mr. Bear didn't.

Mrs. Bear began to snore.
"SNORE," went Mrs. Bear,
"SNORE, SNORE, SNORE."
"Oh NO!" said Mr. Bear,
"I can't stand THIS."
So he got up and went to
sleep in Baby Bear's room.

Baby Bear was not asleep either.
He was lying in bed pretending
to be an aeroplane.
"NYAAOW!" went Baby Bear,
"NYAAOW! NYAAOW!"
"Oh NO!" said Mr. Bear,
"I can't stand THIS."
So he got up
and went to sleep in the living-room.

TICK-TOCK . . . went the living-room
clock. . . . TICK-TOCK, TICK-TOCK.
CUCKOO! CUCKOO!
"Oh NO!" said Mr. Bear,
"I can't stand THIS."
So he went off to sleep in the kitchen.

DRIP, DRIP . . . went the leaky
kitchen tap.
HMMMMMMMMMMMM . . .
went the refrigerator.
"Oh NO," said Mr. Bear,
"I can't stand THIS."
So he got up
and went to sleep in the garden.

Well, you would not believe
what noises there are in
the garden at night.
"TOO-WHIT-TOO-WHOO!"
went the owl.
"SNUFFLE, SNUFFLE," went
the hedgehog.
"MIAAAOW!" sang the cats
on the wall.
"Oh, NO!" said Mr. Bear,
"I can't stand THIS."
So he went off to sleep in
the car.

It was cold in the car
and uncomfortable, but
Mr. Bear was so tired
that he didn't notice.
He was just falling asleep
when all the birds started to
sing and the sun peeped in at
the window.
"TWEET TWEET!" went the birds.
SHINE, SHINE . . . went the sun.
"Oh NO!" said Mr. Bear,
"I can't stand THIS."
So he got up and went back
into the house.

In the house, Baby Bear was
fast asleep, and Mrs. Bear had
turned over and wasn't snoring
any more.
Mr. Bear got into bed and closed his
eyes.
"Peace at last," he said to himself.

BRRRRRRRRRRRRRRR! went the
alarm-clock, BRRRRRR!
Mrs. Bear sat up and rubbed her eyes.
"Good morning, dear," she said.
"Did you sleep well?"
"Not VERY well, dear," yawned
Mr. Bear.
"Never mind," said Mrs. Bear. "I'll
bring you a nice cup of tea."

And she did.